The Lonely Prince

A Story of Acceptance, Friendship, and Love

By Peter D. Weiler

D1410911

Chapter 1: Prince Boka Gets Dethroned

Once upon a time, in a powerful landlocked kingdom named Lorindia [Lo-**rin**-dee-ah], lived a prince named Boka [**Boh**-kah]. Although his mother, the Queen, truly loved him, when he turned five and his brother was born, she had to pay more attention to the baby, and Boka felt neglected and, worse, abandoned.

"Mother, why did you stop loving me when my brother was born?"

"Oh, Boka, I still love you just as much. But I have to pay more attention to the baby now, feeding him and changing his diapers, and I have to share my time with both of you."

"I *know* you don't love me anymore."

Chapter 2: Boka's Grandmother and the Great War

So, Boka would go to his father, the King, to see if he could get some solace.

But his father was a bitter and angry man, who had a terrible childhood, as he was, as a young kid, terrified of his own mother—the former queen and Boka's grandmother. She, too, was full of rage and bitterness, and she took it out on Boka's father.

When his grandmother was a teenager, there arose an evil kingdom—Solandia [So-**lan**-dee-a]. The Solandians' mission was to take over the world and populate it with their own people. They declared everyone else to be inferior, waged wars against all the other kingdoms, and murdered many of their civilians.

But their agenda against Boka's people was especially sinister—they planned to murder them all, and in fact, had murdered a third of them by the end of the war.

Many of the kingdoms who had suffered under Solandia actually hated the Lorindians throughout the ages, so they ended up gladly collaborating with the Solandians. Two of them were Piramia [Pi-**ra**-mee-ah]—where Boka's grandmother was born—and Dimalia [Di-**ma**-lee-ah]. The Dimalians were particularly cruel, as they had been hating the Lorindians for a thousand years before the Solandians ever did.

Whereas many of the Lorindian survivors had other family members who had survived as well, and started their own families, his grandmother's entire family had been murdered, and she was all alone in the world.

Boka's grandfather, who married her eight years after the war was over, and eventually became the Lorindians' king, brought women talk doctors to attempt to help his wife, but they were met with fierce opposition. She felt that she would be betraying her murdered family if she ever felt better.

She engaged Boka's father with ghastly stories of the mass murders of Lorindian civilians that she had witnessed, and it affected him gravely. It made him sad, and together with her state of mind, it made the palace dark and gloomy in spirit.

Boka's mother, however, was always happy and had many friends, though of course, she had to leave the palace to socialize with them. But when Boka's brother was born, a part of her was taken away too, and he felt all alone.

When he approached his father and said, "Father, would you play with me?"

The latter answered, "Boka, look, I did not have it easy growing up either. You see how my mother is. Go make friends with kids your own age."

What the King did not understand was that, since Boka felt abandoned by both his parents, he had developed serious problems connecting with other kids.

In the few times that he did venture out of the palace, for short periods of time, from the age of eight to eleven, he was intimidated by boys, because he felt that they were stronger, and by girls, because they were pretty.

But Boka pined for a girl's company, and because he felt like he had lost his mother, he was willing to be friends with any girl; and he was willing to do some truly reckless things to stop his loneliness.

Chapter 3: Sofia—Boka's Horrible First Friend

Boka was twelve when he met Sofia. He was walking down the street, and she happened to be in front of him. She dropped her handkerchief, and he quickly bent down and picked it up.

"Hey, you dropped this accidentally."

Sofia looked at him in revulsion and said, "It's gross! How dare you hand me a dirty thing like that?"

"I'm sorry. I was just trying to be nice."

Nice, huh? she thought. "My name is Sofia. What's your name?"

"Boka."

"So, do you want to do something together?"

"Sure."

"Well, then you *have* to take me out for ice cream."

"I'd love to."

When they entered the ice cream store and sat down, Boka said excitedly, "I have enough money for four scoops! We can have two scoops each."

"Only two scoops? Either I get four scoops, or I'm leaving!"

"No problem, Sofia. I'll get you four scoops."

"I'm glad you've come to your senses."

Boka ordered four scoops for Sofia and nothing for himself.

"I hope you like it," he said, as she started to eat.

"How dare you? Don't you realize how awkward you make me feel when I'm eating four scoops while you're having nothing?"

Suddenly, out of nowhere, a beautiful girl appeared. She was tall, with light-brown eyes, and light-brown hair in a long braid that started out as a lock of her hair that was parted to the right, went around the back of her neck, and was braided with thick locks as it went around her right shoulder.

She had been watching them the whole time.

"Why do you mistreat your friend like that? He's being nice to you," she said to Sofia indignantly.

"It's none of your business!" said Sofia, glaring at her.

"You mean it's not supposed to be like this?" said Boka.

"No," replied the striking beauty. "Friends are supposed to be pleasant and care about each other."

Boka was flummoxed by the revelation. "Sofia—" he started.

"Fine. I'm leaving." And Sofia stormed out of the store.

Chapter 4: Maruvka Gently Questions Boka

"May I please sit down?"

He nodded.

"What's your name?"

"Boka. What's yours?'

"Maruvka [Mah-**roov**-kah]." She smiled sweetly.

And they shook hands.

"Boka, forgive me, but how did you end up with such an awful girl? I only ask because I care."

"I always wanted to have a girl as a friend, and she was the first one who agreed."

"Oh, Boka, you have to be *really* careful with that," she said passionately. "She sensed how much you wanted friendship, and decided to take advantage of you."

Boka's face fell and he nearly started to cry.

"Do you want to talk about it?" she asked softly.

So, he told her, even though he was embarrassed, how he never got over having a brother, and how his grandmother was so sad and angry all the time, and how his father was also angry and bitter, and how his father had told him to just find friends and lump it. And in general, he described to her how his home was dark and gloomy in spirit.

She looked at him tenderly, smiled and said, "Well, now you have a friend— right here."

Chapter 5: Boka and Maruvka Get to Know Each Other Further

After leaving the ice cream place, they were walking down the street when she asked, "So how far do you live from here?"

"About a 20-minutes' walk."

"And where do you go to school?"

"I get tutored at home."

That's not good. That just increases his isolation, she thought.

"What about you, Maruvka?"

"I go to middle school, and I also attend the conservatorium where I learn how to play the piano. I'd like to play at the capital philharmonic when I grow up. What about you?"

"I'm not sure; whatever it is, it won't be what my father does for a living," he said; and overwhelmed with the day's occurrences he quickly added, "I have to go home."

"Let's meet tomorrow by the ice cream store," she suggested.

Chapter 6: Maruvka Visits the Palace

They hung around each other every day, and after two weeks Maruvka requested, "Can you invite me to your house?"

Oh, no, that would be the last *place where I would want to take anybody.* But then Boka decided to make that brave move, and he agreed.

They walked till they got really close to the palace.

"Are you playing a joke on me?" she smiled.

"Oh, no. Please, let's keep on walking."

As they came by the guards, they said, "Good afternoon, Prince Boka. Who is this young lady?"

"This is my friend, Maruvka."

"Welcome to the royal court, Maruvka."

They both walked through the palace gates.

The first one to greet them was Boka's mother. "Boka, is that your friend?" she said with a smile.

"Yes. Maruvka, this is my mother, the Queen. Mother, this is Maruvka."

"Pleased to meet you," Maruvka said, and they shook hands.

"I'm going to introduce Maruvka to Father."

They both walked towards the King's room.

Boka started noticing that the palace was getting brighter in spirit.

Finally, they reached the King's room.

Boka knocked on the door.

"Who is it?" bellowed the King grumpily.

"It is me, Boka."

The King opened the door abruptly, and he, the King who was always so tough with everyone, smiled widely.

"Maruvka, this is my father, the King. Father, this is my friend, Maruvka."

Maruvka put her hand forward, and he shook it heartily. "Nice to meet you, young lady."

"I feel the same, your liege."

"I am going to take Maruvka to meet grandmother."

They both started for the kitchen, where Boka's grandmother could be found most of the time.

And the palace just kept getting brighter and lighter in spirit.

When they entered the kitchen, Boka accidentally dropped a utensil.

His grandmother turned around with rage, but suddenly, a twinkle came to her eye, and she smiled. Boka had never seen her smile before; it made her look beautiful.

And he introduced them to each other.

As Boka escorted her out of the gate, Maruvka turned to him and said, "Tomorrow?"

"Tomorrow."

Chapter 7: Maruvka Reveals a Terrible Secret to Boka

They kept hanging around each other every day, and about two weeks later, Maruvka knocked on the palace gate. "Boka, let's go to the park and talk a little bit, alright?"

They walked to the park, and Maruvka led him as far away from anyone else as possible.

Suddenly, Maruvka's entire composure changed; she had a serious face. She gazed into his eyes. "Boka, I'm not Lorindian."

"You're not one of us? What people *do* you belong to?"

"I'm Dimalian. My parents immigrated from there when I was five years old."

"You people hate us!" said Boka with revulsion.

"Please, Boka. My parents and I don't feel that way at all."

"I have to go home." He walked away, shaking his head. Then he started to run, and he ran all the way to the palace.

Maruvka cried bitterly. She knew from the moment she saw Boka in the ice cream store that he was different from her—that he was Lorindian. She knew that at some point she would have to reveal her nationality, because secrets are bad. She understood why he reacted that way, but it still hurt her very much.

And Boka thought, *I really can't trust anyone. I thought Maruvka was my friend, and now I find out she's the enemy. It's better to be alone.*

Chapter 8: Boka Gets a Friendly Suggestion from the Palace Guard

Boka had been crying all the way as he ran to the palace, feeling a lot of emotional pain.

When he reached the gate, his friend the palace guard asked, "Boka, what's troubling you?"

So he told him everything: what she had said and how he felt.

"Boka, do you like Maruvka?"

"I do, but I feel bad about it now."

"And do you think she likes you?"

"I *know* she does. But I just don't understand how. Her people have always hated us."

"Boka, we have to give individuals the opportunity to be good, when they truly want it. Go back to the park and talk to her. It'll all work out."

Chapter 9: Boka and Maruvka are Together Again

Boka walked back to the park.

Maruvka was sprawled on her stomach on the grass.

Boka sat down beside her. "Hey, it's me."

Maruvka sat up. Her eyes were red.

"You're a wonderful girl."

"Boka," she said gazing into his eyes. "I knew you were Lorindian the moment I saw you. All I know is that you're a good guy, and that I want us to continue to be friends."

"I do too, Maruvka."

Chapter 10: Maruvka Invites Boka to Meet Her Parents

Two weeks later, Maruvka said, "Boka, my parents would like to meet you."

Boka was nervous. He was going to meet the parents of the girl whom he liked. *Will they ask me uncomfortable questions? What if they don't like me?*

However, Boka overcame his fears, took a warm bath and put on his nicest clothes, and at six in the afternoon, he was at Maruvka's house.

He knocked on the door.

A woman opened the door smiling. "You must be Boka, Maruvka's friend. I'm her mother, Helena. Please, come in."

He entered.

"Oh, Boka, there you are," Maruvka said joyfully.

Suddenly, her father came through the door. "Is that your friend?"

"Yes, this is Boka. Boka, this is my father, Martyn [Maar-**teen**)]. He's a doctor."

"Nice to meet you," they both said at the same time, and shook hands.

"Well, let's sit down and eat," said Helena, and she brought out the meal, which consisted of cabbage leaves stuffed with ground beef and rice.

"It's very tasty, Helena," said Boka.

"Thank you. So, Boka, how far away do you live?"

"About a 40-minutes' walk."

"And what does your father do?" asked Martyn.

"My father is an architect," he lied.

"Oh, nice," said Martyn.

"And what do you do, Helena?" asked Boka.

"I'm a teacher. And your mother?"

"A homemaker," he lied again.

When they were done with the meal, Martyn said, "Maruvka, would you like to play us something on the piano?"

"Sure, Papa."

All of them went to the living room, and with the fireplace crackling comfortingly in the background, Maruvka played lovely music for a while.

"I'll join in," said Martyn, disappearing for a minute and coming back with a violin.

Boka was astounded.

"I'll also pitch in," said Helena, and brought a cello.

And for the next half an hour, they played the most heavenly music together.

"So, all of you play an instrument? Is that a standard thing?"

"Yes. Our people have always valued music very much, and it's very common for our families to have most of their members play instruments. You're welcome to stay longer if you like," said Martyn.

"Thank you," said Boka, who once again was overwhelmed, "but I'll be going home now. I had a great time."

"I'll walk Boka to the street," said Maruvka.

When they left the house, Maruvka said excitedly, "Oh, Boka. They really like you."

And when she returned to her parents, they both smiled, and her mother said, "So your friend is Lorindian—isn't that wonderful!"

Chapter 11: Maruvka Talks to the King About Middle School

A month later, Maruvka said to Boka, "I'd like to discuss with your father the possibility of you going to middle school."

So, Boka got permission, and at the assigned time Maruvka came over.

They all sat down to eat.

His grandmother started serving the meal: a red stew with cubed beef and cubed potatoes, and a cake filled with poppy seeds and raisins, and crepes filled with sweet cream for dessert.

When there was a lull in the conversation, Maruvka spoke up. "So, my liege, why is Boka being tutored at home?"

"In order to protect him from the outside world."

"But that is where we both met. If he came to public school, he would be surrounded by kids his own age, and he would be much happier. Besides, we would get to see each other more."

"Well, alright," said the King.

"And Father, I do not even want the teachers and students to know that I am the prince."

"Fine. I will give the public-school system a chance—for a month," acceded the King.

And both Maruvka and Boka were very grateful.

Chapter 12: Boka's First Day in Middle School

Three days later, when Maruvka came to pick Boka up, he had his backpack on with both arms in the straps.

"So, rule number one: only wear the right strap. It's cool. And this way the kids won't make fun of you."

"You mean there are rules for these things?"

"Of course. But I'll teach you as we go along. Let's get going. The school is about a 20-minutes' walk, and it starts in 15 minutes."

They hurried up and got there on time.

And all the wonderful things that Maruvkah promised the king about the benefits of middle school became true.

Chapter 13: Maruvka and Boka Fall in Love

The days passed quickly and they both turned 16.

One day she turned to him and said, "Boka, how would you like to go on a day trip—just you and me?"

"Oh, absolutely!" he said excitedly.

They took a coach, and within an hour and a half, they were in the countryside.

Maruvka asked the coachman to stop near a huge meadow, and she was determined to take it from there.

They walked around for two hours.

"Let's get some rest. We still have a long day ahead of us," and she lay down in the grass.

Boka was just about to do the same when he had a moment of déjà vu. He recalled the day in the park when Maruvka was so vulnerable and revealed to him her true nationality—the same day he found out that she had known he was Lorindian from the beginning. He also realized how much she had done for him since then.

He sat down and gazed into her eyes lovingly.

She sat up, and that was when they kissed for the very first time.

Chapter 14: Boka Reveals Maruvka's Nationality to His Family

And a month later, Boka decided to do what he had dreaded for the past four years.

One evening, during dinnertime, Boka took a deep breath and said, "Father, Mother, Grandmother, I need to tell you something: Maruvka is not Lorindian."

"This is very serious," said the King. "You know that for thousands of years our people have survived by marrying our own kind only. What people does she belong to?"

"She is Dimalian."

His grandmother went into a rage for the first time since Maruvka had set foot in the palace. "Boka, how can you do this to me? The Dimalians collaborated with the Solandians during the war. Haven't I suffered enough?"

"She and her parents never did anything wrong, and they love and accept our people. And because of her I started being happy, and I am not alone anymore."

"This is not the way I have raised you," said the King. "You are betraying our people!"

Boka stood up and let out a sigh of great anguish, and he left for his room.

Chapter 15: Boka and the Palace Fall into Melancholia

Boka's world collapsed in on him. He was so sad that he did not even have enough energy to put on his pajamas and brush his teeth, but instead he just jumped under the covers and sobbed bitterly.

But what he did not know was that instantly, gloom pervaded the palace again. His grandmother regressed back into her old self, being sad and angry. She raged daily against the King. He himself went back to being sad and angry, too, and he took it out on the Queen. Only the Queen still remained somehow cheerful—even though she suffered greatly.

Boka slept all day, and barely slept at night. He sometimes saw visions of Maruvka, but those quickly faded away, and he would wake up, disappointed that he was still alive.

Chapter 16: Maruvka Finds Out

That entire time, Maruvka was worried sick; Boka had not come to school for two months. She came to the palace many times during that period, but the guards, who had strict directions from the King, would not let her in.

But on one of those occasions, Boka's friend was the guard that day, and he leveled with her.

Chapter 17: Maruvka Takes Action

Maruvka left a note for her parents explaining everything.

She snuck in through a secret passage that went under the palace gate—a passage which both she and Boka had gone through many times, when they were younger. She knocked on his window, which was on the first floor.

Boka opened it, and he was thrilled to see her.

She climbed through the window into his arms.

The color returned to his face, his eyes brightened, and he was happy once more. He had been love sick; and now that Maruvka was back, he knew she would make it better.

Chapter 18: Maruvka Has a Serious Talk with Boka

Now that Boka was happy again, Maruvka engaged him in her plan. "If you come with me, we'll have challenges just to find food and have a roof over our heads."

"The life I've been living the past two months is not a life at all; I want to run away with you."

And they both carefully climbed out the window so as not to make any noise, and they escaped through the secret passage.

Chapter 19: Maruvka and Boka—the Runaways.

They took a coach, and within an hour, they were in the next city. They travelled all night, far away from the palace, where Boka had been melancholic and where Maruvka was not accepted.

They took another coach, and after a week, they realized that they had finally crossed the border. It made them feel safer, as it meant that they were farther from the palace. They were free.

Chapter 20: Boka and Maruvka Settle Down

They found a village and struck up a deal, where they could stay at a little hut and get some food in exchange for herding sheep.

Things went on like that for a while. But Boka noticed that Maruvka was sad sometimes.

One day, he asked, "What's the matter, Maruvka?

"Boka, I really miss my parents; they've always been good to me. But I am glad that we're together again and that you're happy, even though I am hurting."

And Boka realized, once again, how fortunate he was to have such a loving girlfriend.

Chapter 21: The King Finds Boka and Maruvka

The days passed by quickly and both of them turned 18.

And one day, there was a knock on their door. "Boka, please open up. It's your father."

Boka opened the door.

The King was there, and he seemed very despondent.

"Boka, the palace has not been the same without you and Maruvka together. It has been dark and gloomy in spirit again. Your grandmother and I have been sad, once more. And your mother has missed you the entire time."

"You gave Maruvka no chance at all. And you felt so strongly about that, you did not even care that I became melancholic. You practically chased us away."

"I am sorry for the way I acted; it was a big mistake; I admit it. I beg you and Maruvka to come back. I promise, I will accept her like my own daughter."

Boka looked at his father with anger. He was still sore at everything he put him through, and for depriving his girlfriend of her own loving parents. Finally, he said, "I have to talk to Maruvka."

He went inside and told her everything the King said. "I'm just so angry at him; it's hard to forgive what he did."

Maruvka gazed into his eyes, tenderly, and said softly, "It's time to go home."

THE END

About the Author

Peter D. Weiler has also published three other fairytales: *The Anguished Prince: A Fairytale in Reverse*, about bipolar disorder; *The Terrified Prince*, which addresses fears and anxieties, namely Obsessive-Compulsive Disorder (OCD), and the highly sensitive person (HSP), who experiences extreme discomfort, pain, and fear of excessive exposure to the five senses, as well as claustrophobia, and bullying; and *The Sleeping Princess: A Fairytale About Being Up*, about sleep addiction—all of which are available on www.amazon.com. He is currently working on his next fairytale, *The Challenged Prince*.